W9-ABT-007

E
FLY

Flynn saves the day.

$12.99   Preschool   11/01/2011

DATE			

Dear Parent:

Congratulations! Your child is taking the first steps on an exciting journey. The destination? Independent reading!

STEP INTO READING® will help your child get there. The program offers five steps to reading success. Each step includes fun stories and colorful art. There are also Step into Reading Sticker Books, Step into Reading Math Readers, Step into Reading Phonics Readers, Step into Reading Write-In Readers, and Step into Reading Phonics Boxed Sets—a complete literacy program with something to interest every child.

Learning to Read, Step by Step!

Ready to Read   Preschool–Kindergarten
• big type and easy words • rhyme and rhythm • picture clues
For children who know the alphabet and are eager to begin reading.

Reading with Help   Preschool–Grade 1
• basic vocabulary • short sentences • simple stories
For children who recognize familiar words and sound out new words with help.

Reading on Your Own   Grades 1–3
• engaging characters • easy-to-follow plots • popular topics
For children who are ready to read on their own.

Reading Paragraphs   Grades 2–3
• challenging vocabulary • short paragraphs • exciting stories
For newly independent readers who read simple sentences with confidence.

Ready for Chapters   Grades 2–4
• chapters • longer paragraphs • full-color art
For children who want to take the plunge into chapter books but still like colorful pictures.

STEP INTO READING® is designed to give every child a successful reading experience. The grade levels are only guides. Children can progress through the steps at their own speed, developing confidence in their reading, no matter what their grade.

Remember, a lifetime love of reading starts with a single step!

Thomas the Tank Engine & Friends™

CREATED BY BRITT ALLCROFT

Based on The Railway Series by The Reverend W Awdry.
© 2011 Gullane (Thomas) LLC.
Thomas the Tank Engine & Friends and Thomas & Friends are trademarks of
Gullane (Thomas) Limited.
HIT and the HIT Entertainment logo are trademarks of HIT Entertainment Limited.

HIT entertainment

All rights reserved. Published in the United States by Random House Children's Books,
a division of Random House, Inc., 1745 Broadway, New York, NY 10019, and in Canada by
Random House of Canada Limited, Toronto.

Step into Reading, Random House, and the Random House colophon are registered
trademarks of Random House, Inc.

Visit us on the Web!
StepIntoReading.com
www.randomhouse.com/kids
www.thomasandfriends.com

Educators and librarians, for a variety of teaching tools,
visit us at www.randomhouse.com/teachers

ISBN: 978-0-375-86935-8 (trade) — ISBN: 978-0-375-96935-5 (lib. bdg.)

Printed in the United States of America
10 9 8 7 6 5 4 3 2 1

THOMAS & FRIENDS™

Flynn Saves the Day

Based on The Railway Series
by the Reverend W Awdry

Illustrated by Richard Courtney

Random House 🏠 New York

Percy rolls
down the track.

Uh-oh!

Percy smells smoke!

Oh, no!
Percy sees a fire!

Thomas is in trouble!
Who will save him?

Clickety-clack!

Clickety-clack!

Percy finds Flynn.

Flynn is a fire engine.

Flynn is fast.

Flynn is fearless.

Flynn will save Thomas.

Chuff! Chuff!
Clang! Clang!
The engines
hurry to help.

Smoke swirls.
Flames flash.
The engines
work together.

18

Percy clears
the track.
Thomas is free!

Flynn fights the fire.

Whoosh goes the water!

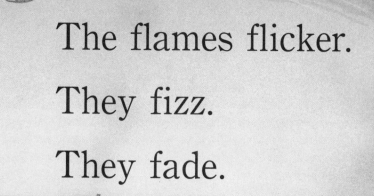

The flames flicker.

They fizz.

They fade.

The fire is out.

Thomas is safe.

"Good job, Flynn!"

"Thank you, Percy!"